Princess Patty

MEETS HER MATCH

Charise Mericle Harper

Disney • HYPERION

LOS ANGELES   NEW YORK

For my dear friend Susan

Princess Patty was waiting
for her prince.
But waiting is not easy.

One Day
Your
Prince
Will Come

"Is one day today?"
asked Princess Patty.

She looked at her pet starfish,
but Miss Loverpuff did not answer;
she was a starfish.

"Oh, fiddlesticks," said the princess.
"I'm tired of waiting. I'll just go find
him myself."

She packed her super-sparkly knapsack with everything she needed and headed out the door.

She could not drive a carriage, she could not ride a horse; but she was wearing her favorite comfy shoes . . . so she walked.

SUPER-COMFY SHOES

"Now I will journey to find my prince,"
declared Princess Patty.

And off she went.

Soon she came to a castle. Inside the castle was a prince. "Are you my prince?" asked Princess Patty.

"Let's see!" said the prince, and in one swift move he grabbed her foot and pulled on her shoe.

"Your shoes have laces!" sobbed the prince. "And they're knotted! I haven't practiced laces!"

"I always make a double knot," said Princess Patty. "Just to be sure my shoes don't fall off."

"What about the glass slipper?" cried the prince. "Don't you want to try it on?"

"It's lovely," said Princess Patty, being polite. "But no, thank you."

And then, because she was thoughtful, she showed the prince how to bend down on one knee and gently hold a foot. She even let him keep her favorite pillow as a cushion for his knee.

Princess Patty waved good-bye and continued on her journey.

Next she came to a big grassy area in front of a small castle. A prince was stomping through the tall grass. "Are you my prince?" shouted Princess Patty.

Thump, thump, thump, the prince came charging over.
"I catch dragons!" bragged the prince. "Do you have a
dragon like this?" He swung his little net in the air.

"Uh-oh," said Princess Patty, pointing. "Those aren't dragons, they're dragonFLIES! Dragons are much bigger and scarier, plus they breathe fire."

dragonfly
(actual size
3 times bigger)

dragon
(actual size
61 times bigger)

"Oh no!" said the prince. "Now I'll have to get a bigger net!"

"Forget the net," said Princess Patty. "You can sneak right past a sleeping dragon if you are as quiet as a mouse."

She showed the prince how to tiptoe, leap, and twirl without making a sound. And then, because she was generous, she let him keep her book of ballet poses so he could practice.

"I've got to stop wasting time," said Princess Patty.
"I have to find my prince! But where? Where is he?
Where could he be?"

Princess Patty walked,
and walked, and walked,
and walked some more.

Finally, she came to another castle. The prince outside looked very happy to see her. "Are you my prince?" she asked cautiously.

"Are you sleepy?" asked the prince.

"Not really," said Princess Patty, "but I am hungry."

"Even after eating the apple?" The prince seemed surprised.

"I haven't eaten an apple," said Princess Patty. "Do you have any?"

"Don't you know how it's supposed to go?" asked the prince. "The witch has the apples! You eat one, fall asleep, and then I kiss you and . . . *Ta-da*, you wake up!"

The prince looked closely at Princess Patty. "I have been practicing my kisses," he said, and he kissed the air and winked at the same time.

"I can see that," said Princess Patty, as she took a step back.

"You have terrible chapped lips."
And then, because she was compassionate,
she gave him her soothing lip balm.

The shoe prince
was not her prince.

The dragon prince
was not her prince.

The kissing prince
was not her prince.

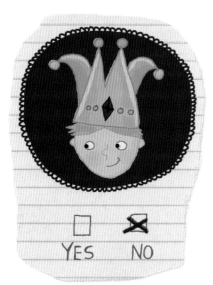

YES　NO

YES　NO

YES　NO

Where was her prince?

Princess Patty marched on. Now
it was getting late, and she was
very hungry. She came to a lovely
castle on top of a little hill.

peas

She looked in the window, and even though she was extra hungry, she snuck away before the prince could see her.

I do not want a prince who keeps his leftovers under his mattress, thought the princess.

Did she have a prince? One that was right just for her? "If it said so on the royal painting, then it must be true," sighed Princess Patty.

She stopped to give Miss Loverpuff a snack, but the starfish food was gone. "Poor Miss Loverpuff! Now you'll be hungry too," said Princess Patty.

Just then a kind peddler came by and offered the princess a ride on his cart. As they traveled, she saw a frog, then another and another.

Could one of them be her prince?

No, she hoped not. Some princesses liked kissing frogs, but she was not one of those.

FREE KISSES

MUSCULAR ARMS

ROCK CLIMBING SHOES

SUPER STRONG HAIR

They rode on and on.
Princess Patty looked up, way up. She saw a prince climbing a tall tower.

"Ouch," said Princess Patty, and she
fluffed her short, stylish pigtails.

Then suddenly the princess saw someone familiar. She thanked the peddler and jumped off the wagon.

"Fairy Godmother! Fairy Godmother!" cried Princess Patty. "Please help me! I can't find my prince."

"Oh dear," said the fairy godmother. "Didn't I just put you in a ball gown and send you off to the royal ball in a carriage made from a pumpkin?"

"No, that wasn't me," said Princess Patty.

"Well, this is embarrassing,"
said the fairy godmother.
"You princesses all look alike.
I just don't know how to keep it
straight."

"When I have too much to remember, I write things down," said Princess Patty.

And then, because she was helpful, she showed the fairy godmother how to make a list.

She even let her keep
the pencil and notebook.

Luckily, Princess Patty's castle
was not far away. She walked home.

She wasn't so sure she wanted a prince after all.

When she got home, there was a tired, ragged prince sitting by the door.

"I'm looking for my princess," he said. "I have been looking all day, but so far I can't find her. If you are my princess you would have to accept that . . ."

"I do not have extra shoes.

I am terrified of dragons.

I do not have magical kisses.

I am scared of heights.

"I have never been a frog,

and I am terribly hungry.

"The only good luck I've had all day is finding this jar of magical star powder—but I think its magic is gone.
So far, nothing has happened to me, and it tastes terrible."

"Perfect," said the princess. "You might just be my prince."

And she was right!

They grew up and lived thoughtfully,
generously, compassionately, and helpfully ever after.
Plus, the prince was a great cook.

First Edition
10 9 8 7 6 5 4 3 2 1
H106-9333-5-14227

Printed in Malaysia

Library of Congress Cataloging-in-Publication Data

Harper, Charise Mericle.
Princess Patty meets her match / Charise Mericle Harper.—First edition.
pages cm
Summary: With no Prince Charming in sight, Princess Patty sets out on a journey to find one for herself.
ISBN-13: 978-1-4231-0804-7
ISBN-10: 1-4231-0804-3
[1. Fairy tales. 2. Princesses—Fiction. 3. Sex role—Fiction. 4. Characters in literature—Fiction] I. Title.
PZ8.H235Pr 2014
[E]—dc23   2013047117

Reinforced binding
Visit www.DisneyBooks.com